D0515947

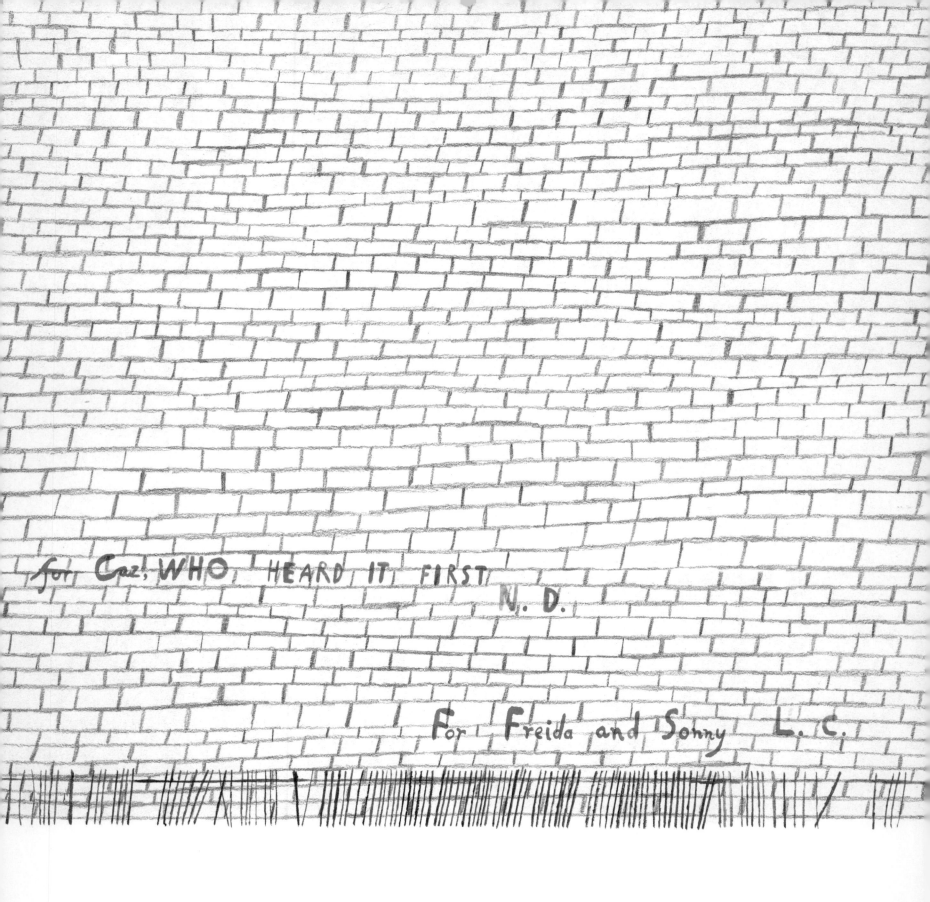

For Caz, WHO HEARD IT FIRST
N. D.

For Freida and Sonny   L. C.

Text copyright © 2013 by Nicola Davies
Illustrations copyright © 2013 by Laura Carlin

All rights reserved. No part of this book may be
reproduced, transmitted, or stored in an information
retrieval system in any form or by any means,
graphic, electronic, or mechanical, including
photocopying, taping, and recording, without
prior written permission from the publisher.

First U.S. edition 2014

Library of Congress
Catalog Card Number 2013934311
ISBN 978-0-7636-6633-0

13 14 15 16 17 18 CCP 10 9 8 7 6 5 4 3 2 1

Printed in Shenzhen, Guangdong, China

This book was typeset in Rockwell.
The illustrations were done in mixed media.

Candlewick Press
99 Dover Street
Somerville, Massachusetts 02144

visit us at www.candlewick.com

MIX
Paper from
responsible sources
FSC
www.fsc.org
FSC® C008047

CANDLEWICK PRESS

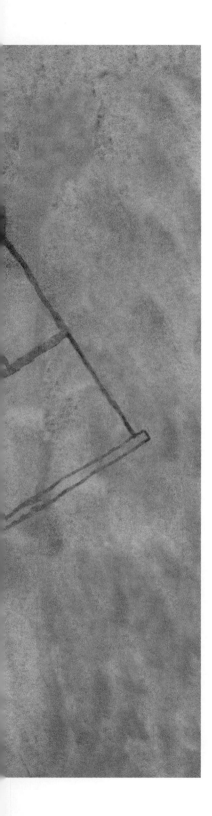

When I was young, I lived in a city

that was mean and hard and ugly.

Its streets were dry as dust,

cracked by heat and cold,

and never blessed with rain.

A gritty yellow wind blew constantly,

scratching around the buildings

like a hungry dog.

Nothing grew. Everything was broken. No one ever smiled.

The people had grown as mean and hard and ugly as their city,
and I was mean and hard and ugly, too.

I lived by stealing from those who had almost as little as I did.

My heart was as shriveled as the dead trees in the park.

And then, one night,

I saw an old lady down a dark street.

She was frail and alone, an easy victim.

Her bag was fat and full,

but when I tried to snatch it from her,

she held on with the strength of heroes.

To and fro we pulled that bag until at last she said,

"If you promise to plant them, I'll let go."

What did she mean? I didn't know or care.

I just wanted the bag, so I said,

"All right, I promise."

She loosened her grip at once and smiled at me.

I ran off without a backward look,
thinking of the food and money in her bag.

But when I opened it . . .
the bag held only acorns.
I stared at them,
so green, so perfect,
and so many,
and I understood

the promise

I had made.
I held a forest in my arms,
and my heart was changed.

I forgot the food and money.
And for the first time in my life, I felt lucky,
rich beyond my wildest dreams.

I slept with the acorns as my pillow,
my head full of leafy visions.

And in the morning, I began to keep

my promise.

I planted beside roads, at rotaries . . .

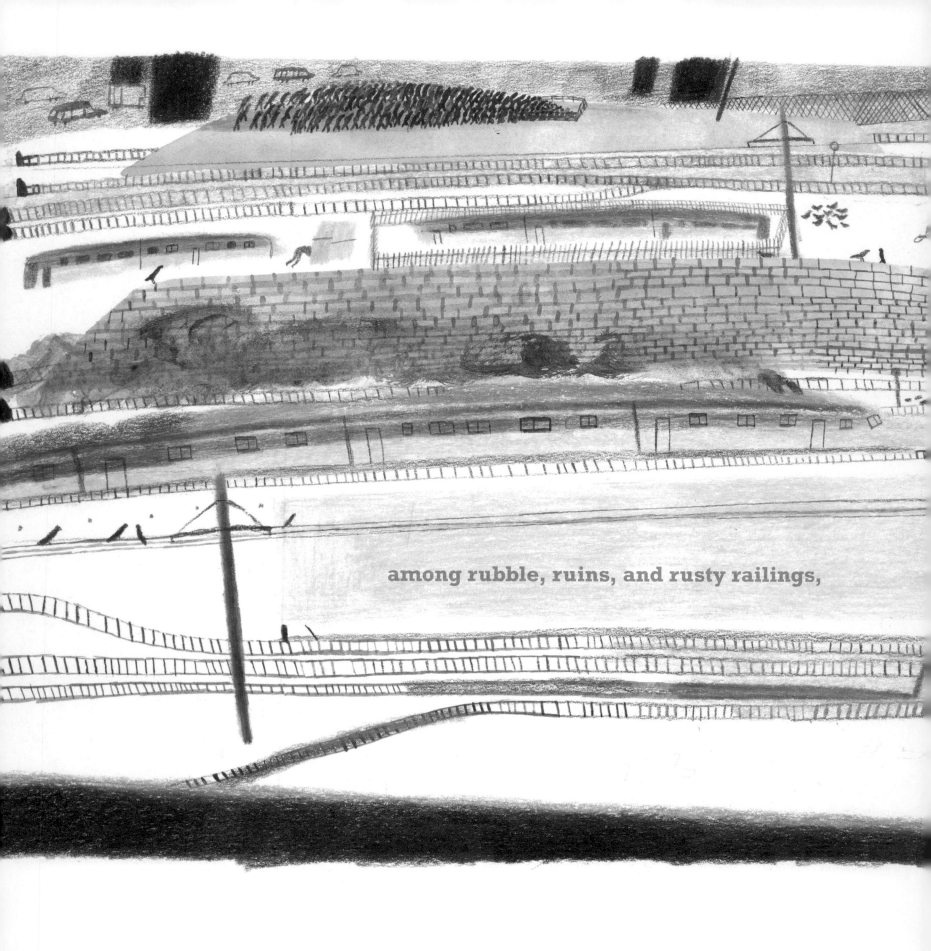

among rubble, ruins, and rusty railings,

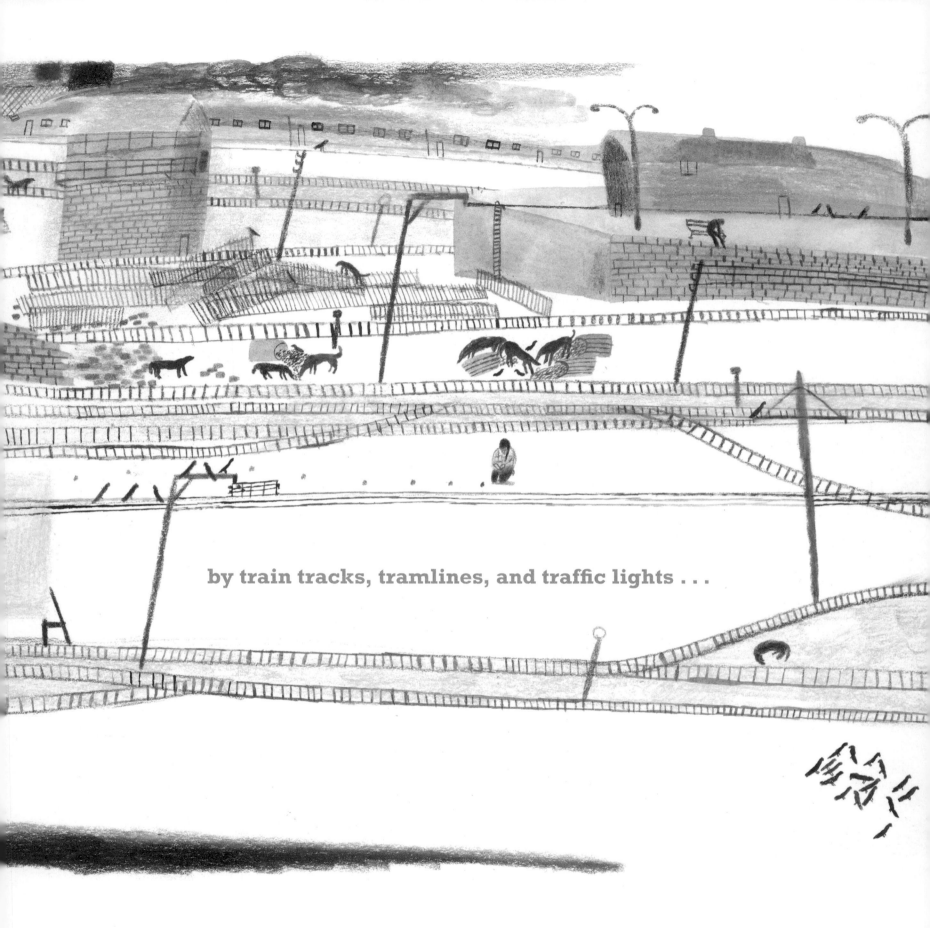

by train tracks, tramlines, and traffic lights . . .

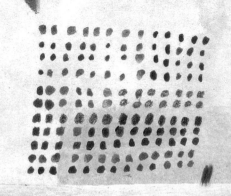

in abandoned parks

and gardens laced with broken glass,

behind factories and shopping malls,

at bus stops, cafés, and apartment buildings.

I pushed aside the mean and hard and ugly,

and I planted, planted, planted.

Nothing changed at first.

The gritty wind still scratched the parched, cracked streets.

The people scowled and scuttled to their homes like cockroaches.

But slowly, slowly, slowly, shoots of green began to show. . . .

TREES!

First here

and there,

then everywhere.

People came onto the streets to see.

They touched the leaves in wonder,
and they smiled.

They had tea together
by the tiny trees.

They talked and laughed . . .

and pretty soon, they were planting, too. Trees and flowers,

fruits and vegetables, in parks and gardens, on balconies and rooftops.

Green spread through the city like a song,

breathing to the sky, drawing down the rain like a blessing.

But by then I was already far away,

planting in another sad and sorry city . . .

and another . . .

and another . . .

and another.

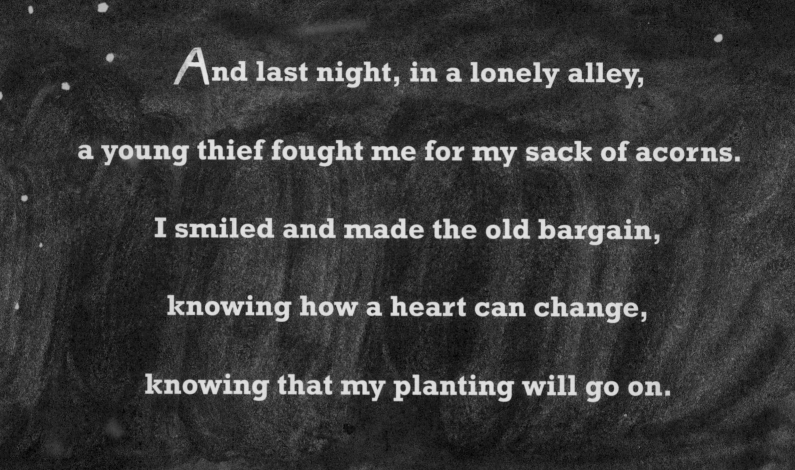

And last night, in a lonely alley,

a young thief fought me for my sack of acorns.

I smiled and made the old bargain,

knowing how a heart can change,

knowing that my planting will go on.